5-MINUTE SUPER HERO STORIES

Scholastic Children's Books, Euston House, 24 Eversholt Street, London NW1 1DB, UK

A division of Scholastic Ltd
London New York Toronto Sydney Auckland
Mexico City New Delhi Hong Kong

This book was first published in the US in 2017 by Scholastic Inc.
This edition published in the UK by Scholastic Ltd, 2018

ISBN 978 14071 8882 9

2 4 6 8 10 9 7 5 3

Printed in China
Papers used by Scholastic Children's Books are made from wood grown in sustainable forests.
www.scholastic.co.uk

TABLE OF CONTENTS

RACE AROUND THE WORLD

IT IS A BRIGHT, SUNNY DAY. AND FOR ONCE, THERE ARE NO SUPER-VILLAINS TO FIGHT.

BUT THAT DOESN'T MEAN ALL IS WELL . . .

SUPERMAN AND THE FLASH ARE HAVING A DISAGREEMENT.

"I'M THE FASTEST!" SAYS SUPERMAN. "I CAN FLY!"

"NO, I'M THE FASTEST," SAYS THE FLASH. "I CAN PRACTICALLY FLY WITHOUT EVEN LEAVING THE GROUND!"

"IT DOESN'T MATTER WHO'S THE FASTEST," SAYS
WONDER WOMAN. "YOU'RE BOTH SUPER HEROES!"
BUT SUPERMAN AND THE FLASH INSIST THEY NEED TO
KNOW.

"HOW ABOUT YOU HAVE A RACE AROUND THE WORLD?" SUGGESTS CYBORG. "WHOEVER FINISHES FIRST WINS!"

SUPERMAN AND THE FLASH LIKE THAT IDEA. THEY GET READY TO RACE!

"DON'T FORGET TO STRETCH," SAYS WONDER WOMAN.

"STRETCHING IS FOR SUPER-VILLAINS," SUPERMAN JOKES. "AND THERE ARE NO SUPER-VILLAINS AROUND TODAY. ONLY SUPER HEROES!"

CYBORG COUNTS DOWN. "THREE . . . TWO . . . ONE . . .
GO!"
SUPERMAN AND THE FLASH ARE OFF!

THEY RACE THROUGH THE CITY. THEY RACE THROUGH THE FIELDS. THEY EVEN RACE OVER THE OCEAN!

SUDDENLY, SUPERMAN HEARS A CRY FOR HELP WITH HIS SUPER-HEARING.

"YOU'RE BLUFFING," SAYS THE FLASH.

BUT SUPERMAN DIVES DEEP INTO THE OCEAN.
HE WAS RIGHT! AQUAMAN IS BATTLING BLACK
MANTA . . . AND SHARKS!

SUPERMAN USES HIS FREEZE BREATH TO ICE BLACK
MANTA AND THE SHARKS ON THE SPOT.
   "THANKS, SUPERMAN," SAYS AQUAMAN. "WAY TO COOL
OFF THOSE BAD GUYS!"
   THEN SUPERMAN BLASTS BACK TO THE RACE.

MEANWHILE, THE FLASH IS STILL RUNNING.

"THERE WAS NO WAY I WAS FALLING FOR SUPERMAN'S BLUFF," HE SAYS. "THERE ARE NO SUPER-VILLAINS TO FIGHT TODAY."

BUT THE FLASH SPOKE TOO SOON . . .

GORILLA GRODD HAS HAWKMAN CORNERED IN THE DESERT!

"NO ONE MONKEYS AROUND WITH MY FRIEND!" CRIES THE FLASH.

THE FLASH SPINS GORILLA GRODD AROUND UNTIL THE EVIL APE IS DIZZY!

"THANKS FOR SAVING ME," SAYS HAWKMAN.

"NO PROBLEM," SAYS THE FLASH. "BUT WATCH OUT. I THINK GORILLA GRODD IS ABOUT TO LOSE HIS BANANAS."

MEANWHILE, SUPERMAN IS FAR AHEAD. BUT USING HIS SUPER-VISION, HE SEES ANOTHER ONE OF HIS FRIENDS IS IN DANGER.

SUPERGIRL NEEDS HELP. BRAINIAC'S SKULL SHIP HAS HER IN ITS GRIP!

"THANKS FOR THE HELP, COUSIN!" SAYS SUPERGIRL. "ANYTIME," SAYS SUPERMAN. "BUT IF YOU'LL EXCUSE ME, I HAVE A RACE TO WIN!"

OUT IN THE FOREST, THE FLASH IS NEARING THE END OF THE RACE. SUDDENLY, HE SPOTS ONE MORE SUPER HERO IN TROUBLE. SINESTRO IS ABOUT TO SMASH GREEN LANTERN WITH A GIANT HAMMER!

"HOW ABOUT A TASTE OF YOUR OWN MEDICINE!" SAYS THE FLASH. HE HAMMERS SINESTRO AWAY WITH A SONIC PUNCH!

"THANKS!" SAYS GREEN LANTERN. "THERE SURE ARE A LOT OF SUPER-VILLAINS OUT TODAY."

"YOU'RE TELLING ME," SAYS THE FLASH. "IT SEEMS LIKE ALL WE'RE DOING IS RACING AROUND BATTLING BAD GUYS!"

JUST THEN, SUPERMAN WHIZZES BY.
"SPEAKING OF RACES, GOTTA GO!" CRIES THE FLASH.

THE RACE IS ALMOST OVER. THE TWO HEROES SPRINT TO THE FINISH LINE!

"FEELING SLUGGISH AFTER FIGHTING ALL THOSE SUPER-VILLAINS?" ASKS SUPERMAN.

"NOT A CHANCE!" SAYS THE FLASH.

SUPERMAN AND THE FLASH FLY ACROSS THE FINISH LINE. IT'S NECK AND NECK! WHO WINS THE RACE?

"IT'S A TIE!" CRIES CYBORG. "YOU BOTH CROSSED THE FINISH LINE AT THE EXACT SAME TIME!"
BOTH HEROES ARE EXHAUSTED.

"OW! CRAMPS!" SAYS THE FLASH.

"I TOLD YOU TWO TO STRETCH FIRST," SAYS WONDER WOMAN, SHAKING HER HEAD.

"I GUESS WE'RE BOTH THE FASTEST!" SUPERMAN LAUGHS.

"AND I'M GLAD WE WERE ABLE TO HELP OUR FRIENDS," SAYS THE FLASH.

"WANT TO RACE AGAIN?" ASKS SUPERMAN.

"ONLY IF YOU PROMISE THERE ARE NO MORE SUPER-VILLAINS TO FIGHT ALONG THE WAY!" SAYS THE FLASH. "BUT IF THERE ARE. . . THEY'LL HAVE A TOUGH TIME BEATING THE TWO OF US!"

THE END.

S'MORE SURPRISES

LOOK! UP IN THE SKY! IT'S A BIRD! IT'S A PLANE! IT'S SUPERMAN!

SUPERMAN IS ONE OF THE STRONGEST HEROES IN
THE UNIVERSE. HE HAS INCREDIBLE POWERS! HE CAN FLY
SUPER-FAST.

"UP, UP, AND AWAY!" CRIES SUPERMAN.

HE CAN CARRY HEAVY OBJECTS WITH HIS SUPER-STRENGTH.

"NEED A LIFT?" HE ASKS, PULLING A BUS OUT OF DANGER IN THE NICK OF TIME.

"THANK YOU FOR SAVING US FROM GETTING CRUSHED!"
CRY THE CITIZENS.

HE'S FAST ENOUGH TO SAVE A CAR FROM GETTING HIT BY
A SPEEDING TRAIN.

"ALWAYS REMEMBER TO LOOK BOTH WAYS BEFORE
CROSSING THE TRACKS," HE TELLS THE DRIVER.

WITH HIS X-RAY VISION, SUPERMAN CAN MAKE SURE ALL THE MONEY IN A BANK SAFE IS STILL THERE.

"NINE HUNDRED NINETY-EIGHT, NINE HUNDRED NINETY-NINE, ONE THOUSAND," COUNTS SUPERMAN.

HE CAN EVEN USE HIS FREEZE BREATH TO
PUT BAD GUYS ON ICE!
SUPERMAN IS ONE COOL DUDE.

OF COURSE, ONE OF SUPERMAN'S BIGGEST STRENGTHS IS THE HELP OF HIS SUPER HERO FRIENDS.

"WITH TEAMMATES LIKE YOU, I ALMOST DON'T NEED SUPERPOWERS," HE TELLS WONDER WOMAN.

"BUT WE'RE GLAD YOU HAVE THEM," SAYS WONDER WOMAN.

AND IF THERE'S ONE THING THAT SUPERMAN ENJOYS EVEN MORE THAN USING HIS POWERS TO STOP BAD GUYS . . .

IT'S HAVING A REALLY FUN TIME WITH HIS FRIENDS!

"CANNONBALL!" CRIES SUPERMAN.

"HA, YOU CALL THAT A SPLASH?" TEASES AQUAMAN.
"LET THE KING OF THE SEVEN SEAS SHOW YOU HOW IT'S
DONE."

OF COURSE, SUPERMAN SOMETIMES GETS A LITTLE
CARRIED AWAY WITH THE FUN . . .

"HEY, NO FAIR!" CRIES AQUAMAN. "IT'S NOT COOL TO
FREEZE THE KING OF THE SEVEN SEAS!"

BUT WHENEVER THERE'S TROUBLE, THE SUPER HEROES CAN ALWAYS COUNT ON SUPERMAN TO COME TO THEIR AID.

"SUPERMAN, COME QUICK!" CRIES THE FLASH. "THERE'S A MYSTERIOUS PILE OF BRICKS IN THE PARK, AND I THINK SOMEONE IS TRAPPED INSIDE!"

THE FLASH ZIPS UP TO THE LARGE PILE OF BRICKS.
"SEE?" HE SAYS. "THERE'S NO WAY IN, AND I SMELL
SMOKE COMING FROM INSIDE. THERE MUST BE SOMEONE
TRAPPED IN THERE!"

"LEAVE IT TO ME," SAYS SUPERMAN. WITH A BRIGHT FLASH, HE USES HIS HEAT VISION TO BLAST AWAY SOME OF THE BRICKS.

"WE CAN HELP, TOO," CRIES GREEN LANTERN. HE USES HIS POWER RING TO CREATE A GREEN FIST AND PUNCHES AWAY ANOTHER CHUNK OF BRICKS.

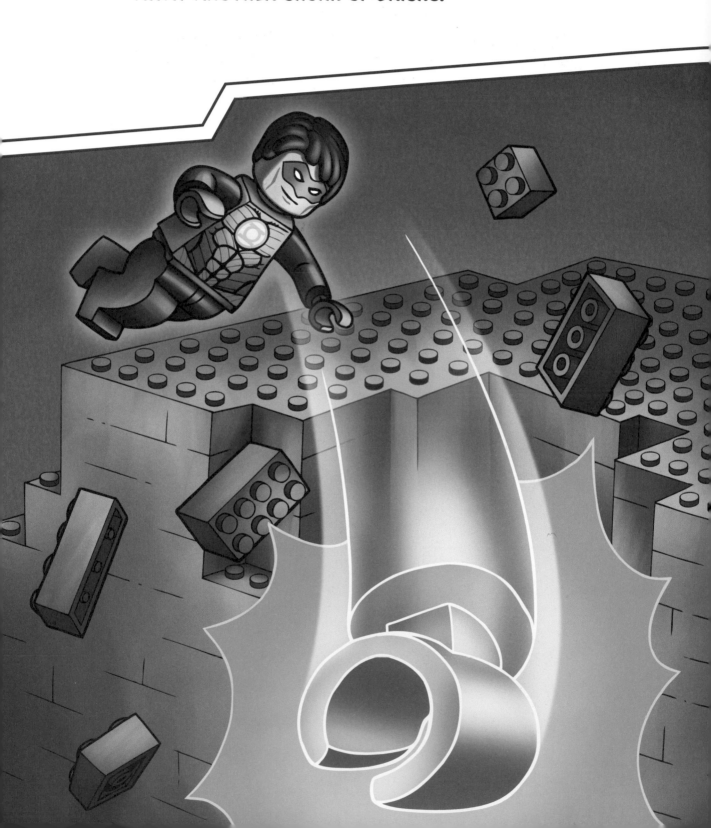

"NOW YOU'RE TALKING," SAYS WONDER WOMAN. "I KNOW HOW TO PACK A PUNCH, TOO!" SHE KNOCKS AWAY EVEN MORE BRICKS. THE SUPER HEROES ARE ALMOST THROUGH!

"COME ON, TEAM," SAYS SUPERMAN. "WE HAVE TO
WORK TOGETHER!"

USING THEIR COMBINED STRENGTH, THE SUPER
HEROES BLAST AWAY THE REST OF THE BRICKS!

"WHO IS TRAPPED INSIDE?" ASKS THE FLASH.

THE FRIENDS ARE IN FOR A BIG SURPRISE . . .

IT'S BATMAN AND ROBIN, HAVING A CAMPOUT!

"YOU DIDN'T NEED TO BREAK APART OUR BRICK TENT," SAYS BATMAN. "YOU COULD HAVE JUST KNOCKED."

"BUT YOU'RE JUST IN TIME!" SAYS ROBIN. "COME GRAB A STICK—WE'RE TOASTING MARSHMALLOWS!"

"NOW *THIS* IS WHAT I CALL FUN," SAYS SUPERMAN.
HE TOASTS A MARSHMALLOW USING HIS HEAT VISION.
"S'MORES, ANYONE?"

THE END.

CATCH THAT CATWOMAN!

HIGH ABOVE GOTHAM CITY, A LONE FIGURE LOOKS OUT FROM ON TOP OF A TALL BUILDING. WHO IS THIS MASKED HERO STANDING GUARD IN THE MIDDLE OF THE NIGHT?

IT'S BATMAN, OF COURSE!

SUDDENLY, THE BAT-SIGNAL LIGHTS UP. SOMEONE NEEDS BATMAN'S HELP!

THE CAPED CRUSADER RACES BACK TO THE BATCAVE. WITH HIS BATCOMPUTER, HE CAN FIND OUT WHERE THE BAD GUYS ARE STRIKING ANYTIME, ANYWHERE.

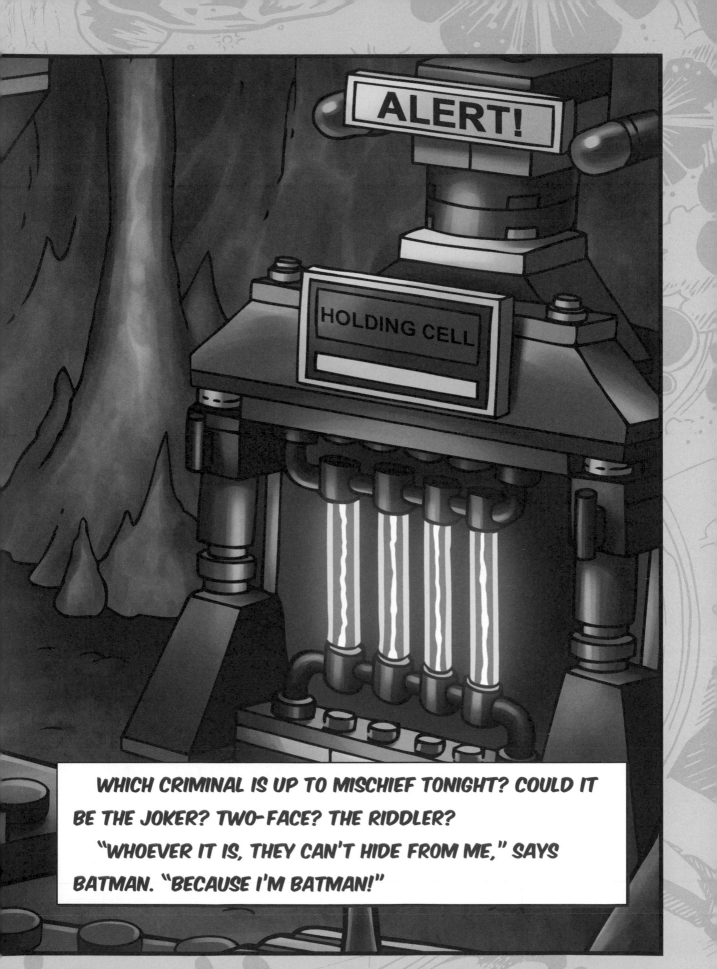

WHICH CRIMINAL IS UP TO MISCHIEF TONIGHT? COULD IT BE THE JOKER? TWO-FACE? THE RIDDLER?

"WHOEVER IT IS, THEY CAN'T HIDE FROM ME," SAYS BATMAN. "BECAUSE I'M BATMAN!"

ROBIN COMES TO THE BATCAVE TO HELP. "THE
COMPUTER SAYS THAT CATWOMAN IS ON THE PROWL AT
THE GOTHAM JEWELRY STORE."

"THEN WE HAVE A CAT TO CATCH," SAYS BATMAN. "AND
FAST!"

BATMAN HAS LOTS OF FAST VEHICLES. THERE'S THE
BATPLANE. AND THE BATBOAT.
BUT TONIGHT, HE'LL USE THE BATCYCLE!

BATMAN ALSO HAS LOTS OF GADGETS. HE HAS THE BAT-CUFFS. AND HIS BINOCULARS.

FOR THIS MISSION, HE'LL USE THE BATARANG!

"PERFECT," SAYS BATMAN. "I HAVE MY RIDE, AND I HAVE MY GADGET. NOW ALL I NEED IS . . ."

. . . A PEANUT-BUTTER-AND-JELLY SANDWICH?
"EVEN SUPER HEROES HAVE TO EAT," HE TELLS
ROBIN. "AND I CAN TAKE THIS MEAL TO GO!"

MEANWHILE, DOWNTOWN, CATWOMAN HAS GOTTEN HER CLAWS ON A BIG DIAMOND FROM THE GOTHAM JEWELRY STORE. "MEOW," SHE SAYS. "COME HERE, MY PET!"
"STOP RIGHT THERE!" YELLS A SECURITY GUARD.

"SORRY," SAYS CATWOMAN. "BUT THIS DIAMOND WILL LOOK PURRRRRFECT WITH MY NEW OUTFIT. TIME FOR ME TO HIGHTAIL IT OUT OF HERE!"

CATWOMAN ZIPS AWAY ON HER MOTORBIKE.
CRASH! SHE SLAMS INTO A FIRE HYDRANT.
SMASH! SHE KNOCKS OVER A MAILBOX.
"SORRY ABOUT THE MESS," SHE CALLS TO A POLICE
OFFICER. "BUT THIS FELINE LIKES TO GO FAST."

IT LOOKS LIKE CATWOMAN IS GOING TO GET AWAY!
BUT SHE DOESN'T NOTICE THE BAT-SIGNAL BLAZING IN THE
NIGHT SKY . . .

BATMAN ZOOMS UP ALONGSIDE CATWOMAN ON HIS BATCYCLE!

"PLAYTIME IS OVER, CATWOMAN," BATMAN SAYS. "YOUR NINE LIVES HAVE OFFICIALLY RUN OUT!"

"TSK, TSK, BATMAN," SAYS CATWOMAN. "YOU'LL NEVER PUT A LEASH ON THIS KITTY!"

CATWOMAN SPEEDS OFF AGAIN, LEAVING A TRAIL OF
DUST BEHIND HER!

BUT BATMAN HAS A CLEVER PLAN. HE USES HIS
BATARANG TO SNARE THE SNEAKY KITTY!
"TRY THIS ON FOR SIZE," HE SAYS.

CATWOMAN GETS TANGLED IN THE BATARANG'S ROPE AND CRASHES INTO A FIRE HYDRANT. WATER GOES EVERYWHERE!

"MEOW!" CATWOMAN CRIES ANGRILY. "DIDN'T ANYONE EVER TELL YOU THAT CATS DON'T LIKE TO GET WET?"

"OH, DON'T WORRY," SAYS BATMAN. "I KNOW A PLACE THAT WILL BE NICE AND DRY, JUST FOR YOU . . ."

"... YOUR JAIL CELL!" SAYS BATMAN.

"RATS," SAYS CATWOMAN. "WHAT A CAT-TASTROPHE THIS HEIST TURNED OUT TO BE."

THE END.

SIDEKICK SHOWDOWN!

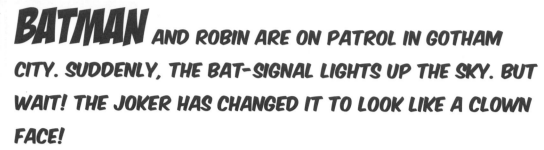

BATMAN AND ROBIN ARE ON PATROL IN GOTHAM CITY. SUDDENLY, THE BAT-SIGNAL LIGHTS UP THE SKY. BUT WAIT! THE JOKER HAS CHANGED IT TO LOOK LIKE A CLOWN FACE!

"LOOKS LIKE THE JOKER IS UP TO HIS USUAL TRICKS,"
SAYS ROBIN, TRYING TO HIDE HIS LAUGHTER.
"IT'S NOT FUNNY!" SAYS BATMAN.

BATMAN AND ROBIN FLY TO THE ROOF WHERE THE
BAT-SIGNAL IS.
OH, NO! THE JOKER AND HIS PALS HAVE CAPTURED
CYBORG AND AQUAMAN.

"WE HAVE TO SAVE THEM!" SAYS BATMAN. "BUT IT'S TWO AGAINST THREE! I'LL CALL FOR BACKUP."

ALL THE SUPER HEROES SWOOP DOWN TO HELP.
WONDER WOMAN PLANTS HER LASSO AROUND
POISON IVY. SUPERMAN FREEZES THE PENGUIN IN
HIS TRACKS. AND BATMAN KNOCKS THE JOKER
OUT WITH A PIE.

"HEY, THROWING PIES IS MY THING!"
COMPLAINS THE JOKER.

THE HEROES HAVE SAVED THE DAY ONCE AGAIN!

"CAN I FLY THE BATCOPTER HOME?" ASKS ROBIN.

"NO," SAYS BATMAN. "SIDEKICKS ARE TOO YOUNG TO FLY."

MEANWHILE, HARLEY QUINN ARRIVES HOME TO FIND THE JOKER MISSING.

"DON'T WORRY, MR. J. I'LL SAVE YOU!" SHE CRIES.

77

HARLEY CALLS CROC AND CAPTAIN BOOMERANG TO COME HELP HER ROUND UP THE SUPER HEROES. THEY CAPTURE BATMAN, WONDER WOMAN, AND SUPERMAN!

"TELL ME WHERE MR. J IS, OR ELSE!" THREATENS HARLEY.

"WE'LL NEVER TELL YOU HE'S IN ARKHAM ASYLUM!" SHOUTS SUPERMAN FROM HIS CAGE.

HARLEY HOPS ON HER MOTORCYCLE AND TAKES OFF.
SHE'LL HAVE THE JOKER FREE IN NO TIME!

MEANWHILE, ROBIN HAS FOUND BATMAN AND THE OTHER HEROES TRAPPED IN A WAREHOUSE.

"I'LL FLY THE BATCOPTER IN TO SAVE YOU!" SAYS ROBIN.

"NO, YOU'RE STILL TOO YOUNG," SAYS BATMAN. "YOU NEED TO STOP HARLEY BEFORE SHE FREES THE JOKER FROM ARKHAM ASYLUM."

AT FIRST, ROBIN ISN'T SURE WHAT TO DO. BUT THEN HE REMEMBERS WHAT BATMAN DID—HE CALLED HIS FRIENDS FOR HELP!

ROBIN ASKS TWO MORE SIDEKICKS, BATGIRL AND SUPERGIRL, TO HELP HIM SAVE THE DAY.

OUTSIDE ARKHAM ASYLUM, HARLEY QUINN, CAPTAIN
BOOMERANG, AND CROC ARE WAITING.

"LOOK, FELLAS." HARLEY LAUGHS. "A LITTLE BIRDIE
DROPPED IN. AND HE BROUGHT ALONG HIS CHICKADEE
FRIENDS!"

"WE'LL SEE WHO THE BIRDIES ARE WHEN YOU JAILBIRDS ARE SENT BACK TO ROOST," SAYS ROBIN.

"THREE AGAINST THREE—DIVIDE AND CONQUER?" SAYS BATGIRL.

"SURE," SAYS SUPERGIRL. "I'LL TAKE BIG, GREEN, AND SCALY!"

ROBIN LEAPS UP AND OVER HARLEY'S HAMMER.
BATGIRL DODGES THE CAPTAIN'S BOOMERANGS.
SUPERGIRL FIGHTS CROC WITH HER SUPER-STRENGTH.

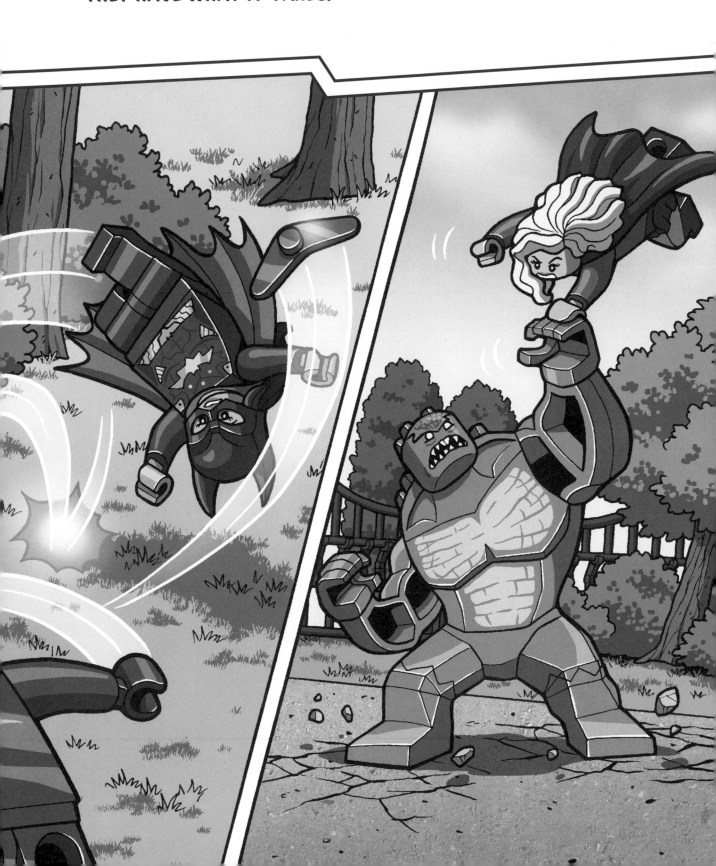

THESE SIDEKICKS SURE ARE SHOWING THE BAD GUYS
THEY HAVE WHAT IT TAKES!

NOW IT'S TIME FOR THE SIDEKICKS TO WRAP UP THE FIGHT.

ROBIN THROWS HIS CAPE OVER HARLEY'S FACE. "LIGHTS OUT!" HE SAYS.

BATGIRL'S BATARANG HITS ITS MARK. "IT'S CALLED A
BATARANG FOR A REASON," SHE SAYS.

AND IT TURNS OUT, CROC IS SUPER TICKLISH! "WHO'S A
BIG, TICKLISH CROCODILE? YOU ARE!" CRIES SUPERGIRL.

THE SIDEKICKS TAKE THE BAD GUYS TO JAIL. IT LOOKS LIKE THEIR WORK IS DONE.

"I HOPE THEY HAVE TACO TUESDAYS IN JAIL," SAYS CAPTAIN BOOMERANG.

"YOU WERE SUPPOSED TO RESCUE ME, NOT *JOIN* ME!"
THE JOKER TELLS HARLEY.

BACK AT THE WAREHOUSE, THE SIDEKICKS FREE THEIR FRIENDS.

"GREAT JOB, YOU THREE," SAYS SUPERMAN.

"YES, WE'RE VERY THANKFUL," SAYS WONDER WOMAN.

BATMAN GRUMBLES. HE IS NOT SURE IF HE'S THAT THANKFUL.

BUT HE SUPPOSES ROBIN DESERVES A TREAT FOR ALL HIS HARD WORK.

"OKAY, MAYBE JUST THIS ONCE," HE SAYS.

"SAVING THE DAY WAS FUN!" SAYS ROBIN. "BUT FLYING THE BATCOPTER IS THE MOST FUN OF ALL!"

THE END.

TOO MANY CROOKS

ONE EVENING IN GOTHAM CITY, BATMAN IS ON HIS WAY TO THE BANK.

"SEEMS TO BE A QUIET NIGHT," HE SAYS. "SO NOW IS THE PERFECT TIME TO PUT SOME MONEY IN MY SAFE."

BATMAN SPOKE TOO SOON. THERE'S A RACKET
DOWNTOWN.

IT'S TWO-FACE! THE TWO-TIMING CROOK IS USING A
CRANE TO BREAK INTO THE BANK!

"HEH, HEH, HEH," LAUGHS TWO-FACE. "THE BANK'S MONEY MAY BE SAFE IN THE SAFE, BUT THE BANK ISN'T SAFE FROM MY CRANE!"

TWO-FACE SMASHES INTO THE BANK AND USES HIS CRANE TO STEAL THE SAFE!

"I GOT WHAT I CAME FOR," HE SAYS. "NOW TO MAKE THE PERFECT GETAWAY!"

"THE ONLY GETAWAY YOU'LL BE MAKING IS A TRIP TO ARKHAM ASYLUM!" YELLS BATMAN.

"YOU'LL NEVER CATCH ME, YOU BUMBLING BAT!" CRIES
TWO-FACE.

WHOOPS. TWO-FACE ISN'T WATCHING WHERE HE'S GOING.

CRASH! HE SLAMS INTO A BRICK WALL! THE SAFE GOES
FLYING.

"I'LL TAKE THAT SAFE," SAYS BATMAN. "AND THE POLICE
WILL TAKE YOU."

TWO-FACE IS FEELING DIZZY FROM HIS CRASH. "WHY AM I
SEEING DOUBLE?" HE ASKS.

"THANK YOU FOR STOPPING THAT TWO-TIMING CROOK!" CRY THE POLICE OFFICERS.

"I WAS ACTUALLY ON MY WAY TO PUT SOME MONEY IN THE SAFE," SAYS BATMAN. "BUT I NEEDED TO SAVE THE SAFE FIRST!"

"YOU'LL PAY FOR THIS," CRIES TWO-FACE. "AND I DON'T MEAN WITH MONEY. BANE AND POISON IVY ARE CAUSING TROUBLE ON THE OTHER SIDE OF TOWN—THEY'LL TAKE CARE OF YOU FOR ME!"

"IS THAT SO?" SAYS BATMAN. "THANKS FOR THE TIP.
TWO CROOKS FOR THE PRICE OF ONE."
    BATMAN USES HIS UTILITY BELT TO SUMMON HIS
BATCYCLE. AND HE'S OFF!

"WELCOME TO THE GARDEN PARTY," POISON IVY SAYS TO BATMAN WHEN HE ARRIVES. "WHAT BUSY BEE TOLD YOU WHAT WE WERE UP TO?"

UH-OH. BANE IS PLANNING TO DRIVE HIS TANK INTO GOTHAM CITY HALL. AND BATMAN CAN'T STOP HIM WITH HIS SMALL BATCYCLE . . .

BATMAN CHASES BANE IN HIS BATPLANE, AND
THE NO-GOOD BAD GUY CRASHES INTO TWO PARKED
MOTORBIKES!

"HOW ABOUT THAT," SAYS BATMAN. "A MOTORBIKE
STOPPED YOUR BIG TANK AFTER ALL."

"LAUGH ALL YOU WANT NOW, BATMAN," SAYS BANE.
"BUT YOU WON'T BE LAUGHING WHEN YOU FIND OUT WHAT
MR. FREEZE HAS PLANNED FOR YOUR FRIEND AQUAMAN."

"ANOTHER CROOK IS ON THE LOOSE?" BATMAN GROANS.
"AND I THOUGHT TONIGHT WAS GOING TO BE PEACEFUL AND
RELAXING."

BATMAN RACES OFF TO HELP AQUAMAN IN HIS BATBOAT. HE BRINGS ROBIN ALONG TO HELP.

"I THOUGHT YOU SAID THERE WEREN'T ANY CROOKS TO CATCH TONIGHT," SAYS ROBIN. "I WAS WATCHING TV!"

"I WAS WRONG," SAID BATMAN. "THERE ARE DEFINITELY TOO MANY CROOKS OUT TONIGHT."

FROZEN ICE POPS! MR. FREEZE HAS TRAPPED AQUAMAN
IN A GIANT BLOCK OF ICE!
"HA, HA." MR. FREEZE LAUGHS. "JUST HOW I LIKE MY
FISH—FROZEN!"

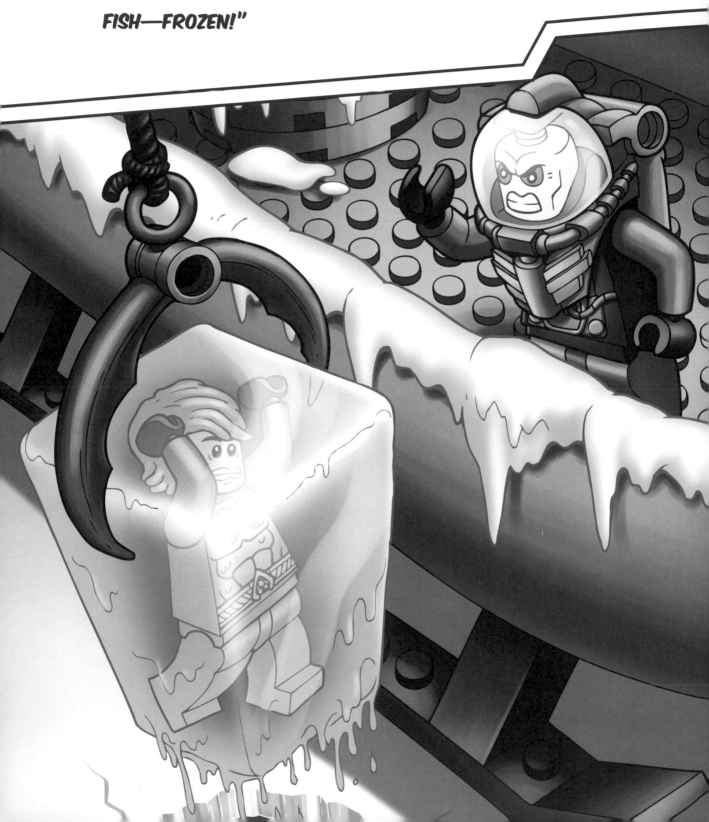

"SORRY, MR. FREEZE," SAYS BATMAN. "BUT I DON'T LIKE MY FISH FROZEN. I LIKE THE BAD GUYS ON ICE AND MY FRIENDS TO BE FREE!"

BATMAN USES THE BATBOAT'S HEAT-BLAST CANNON TO MELT THE ICE AND FREE AQUAMAN!

"DRAT!" YELLS MR. FREEZE. "MY PLAN IS RUINED! HOW DID YOU TWO CAPED DO-GOODERS EVEN KNOW WHAT I WAS UP TO ANYWAY?"

BATMAN SMILES. "LET'S JUST SAY TOO MANY CROOKS SPOIL THE SECRET."

THE END.

CARNIVAL CAPERS!

ONE EVENING, BATMAN AND ROBIN HEAD DOWN TO THE BATCAVE. SUDDENLY, THEY HEAR A NOISE.

OH, NO! WHAT COULD THAT SOUND BE? IS THE DYNAMIC DUO IN TROUBLE?

"AW, MAN, *I* WANT TO ADD THE FROSTING!" ROBIN JOINS IN THE SCUFFLE.

"YOU CAN'T *ALL* BE ON FROSTING DUTY," BATMAN SAYS. "YOU HAVE TO PRACTICE WORKING TOGETHER AS A TEAM. TEAMWORK IS MORE POWERFUL THAN ANY GIZMO IN YOUR UTILITY BELT."

ALFRED HAS AN IDEA. "PERHAPS A BREAK IS IN ORDER," HE SAYS. "MAYBE MASTER ROBIN AND HIS FRIENDS WOULD LIKE TO INVESTIGATE THAT MYSTERIOUS NEW CARNIVAL IN TOWN?"

"OH, BOY, WOULD WE!" CRY ROBIN, STARFIRE, AND BEAST BOY.

BATMAN TAKES THE YOUNG SUPER HEROES TO THE GOTHAM PIER CARNIVAL.

"REMEMBER, DON'T SPLIT UP," HE SAYS. "STICK TOGETHER AS A TEAM!"

MEANWHILE, ROBIN PASSES BY A DUNK TANK.
"TRY YOUR LUCK AND THROW THE BALL," CRIES THE
ATTENDANT. "THIS IS THE FUNNIEST GAME OF ALL!"

ON THE OTHER SIDE OF THE CARNIVAL, BEAST BOY FINDS A DUCKY RIDE.

"STEP RIGHT UP AND RIDE THE DUCK!" CALLS THE CARNIVAL WORKER.

"AWESOME!" SAYS BEAST BOY. "HOW MANY TICKETS?"

OH, NO! IT'S A TRAP! THOSE WEREN'T CARNIVAL WORKERS—THEY'RE SUPER-VILLAINS! AND THEY'VE CAPTURED ROBIN, STARFIRE, AND BEAST BOY!

"WITH YOU THREE TIED UP, WE CAN RIDE ALL THE RIDES WE WANT!" THE JOKER LAUGHS.

THE YOUNG SUPER HEROES NEED TO FIGURE A WAY OUT OF THIS!

"BATMAN TOLD US TO WORK TOGETHER," ROBIN WHISPERS. "AND THAT'S WHAT WE NEED TO DO! BEAST BOY, PRESS THE ALARM ON THE BACK OF MY UTILITY BELT."

BACK IN THE BATCAVE, BATMAN GETS THE SIGNAL. "ROBIN NEEDS HELP," HE SAYS. "I'LL CALL MY FRIENDS."

THE JOKER LAUGHS EVILLY. "NO ONE CAN SAVE YOU NOW, KIDDOS!"

"THAT'S WHAT YOU THINK," SAYS ROBIN.

JUST THEN, ALL THE SUPER HEROES ZOOM TO THE RESCUE!

"THE JOKE IS ON US!" CRIES THE JOKER. "RUN AWAY!"

"EVERY VILLAIN FOR HERSELF!" SHOUTS HARLEY.

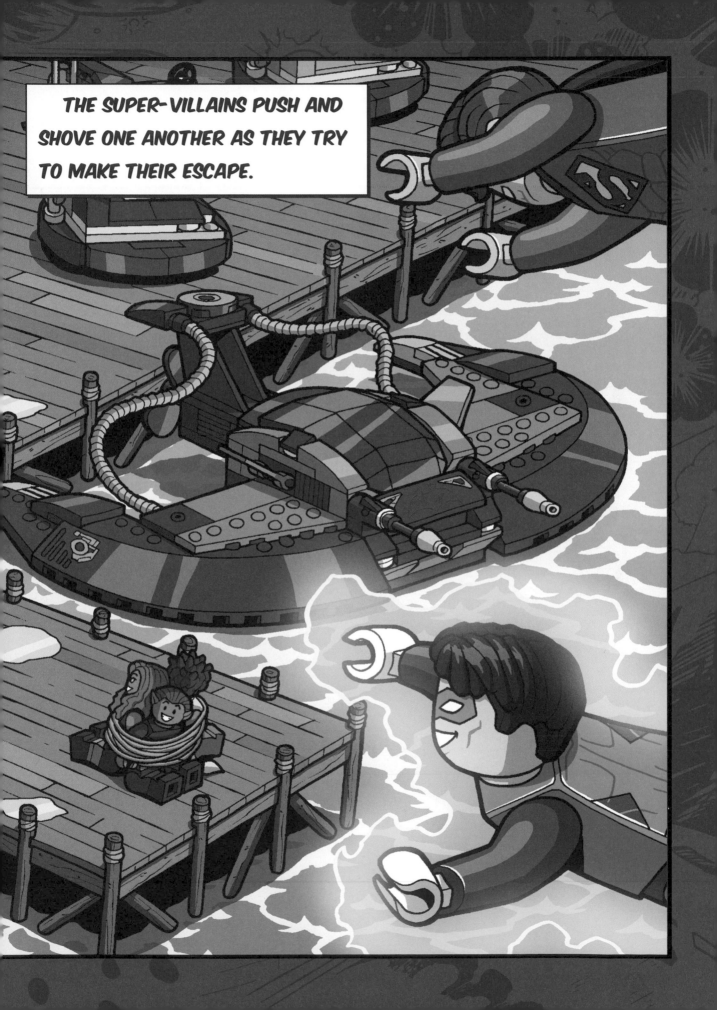

THE SUPER-VILLAINS PUSH AND SHOVE ONE ANOTHER AS THEY TRY TO MAKE THEIR ESCAPE.

THE SUPER-VILLAINS ARE ALL SPLIT UP, BUT THE GOOD GUYS WORK TOGETHER AS A TEAM.

"SORRY, BLACK MANTA, BUT THERE'S NO COTTON CANDY IN JAIL," SAYS NIGHTWING.

SUPERGIRL USES HER FREEZE BREATH TO SLIP UP POISON IVY. "HASN'T ANYONE EVER TOLD YOU? FROST ISN'T GOOD FOR PLANTS," SHE SAYS.

HARLEY QUINN TRIES TO ESCAPE ON THE BUMPER CARS.

BUT AQUAMAN AND THE FLASH PUT THE BRAKES ON HER PLAN!

AND WONDER WOMAN AND SUPERMAN NAB
THE PENGUIN.

"TOUGH LUCK, PENGUIN," SAYS SUPERMAN.
"BUT YOUR PLAN WAS NEVER GOING TO FLY."

THE SUPER-VILLAINS ARE ALL CAPTURED . . . EXCEPT FOR THE JOKER!

"WE'RE ON IT!" CRY HAWKMAN AND GREEN LANTERN.

SOON, THE JOKER IS SEEING GREEN WHEN THE HEROES STOP HIS STEAMROLLER IN ITS TRACKS!

THE SUPER-VILLAINS' PLAN HAS BEEN FOILED!
"THE FUN AND GAMES ARE OVER FOR YOU CROOKS,"
SAYS WONDER WOMAN.

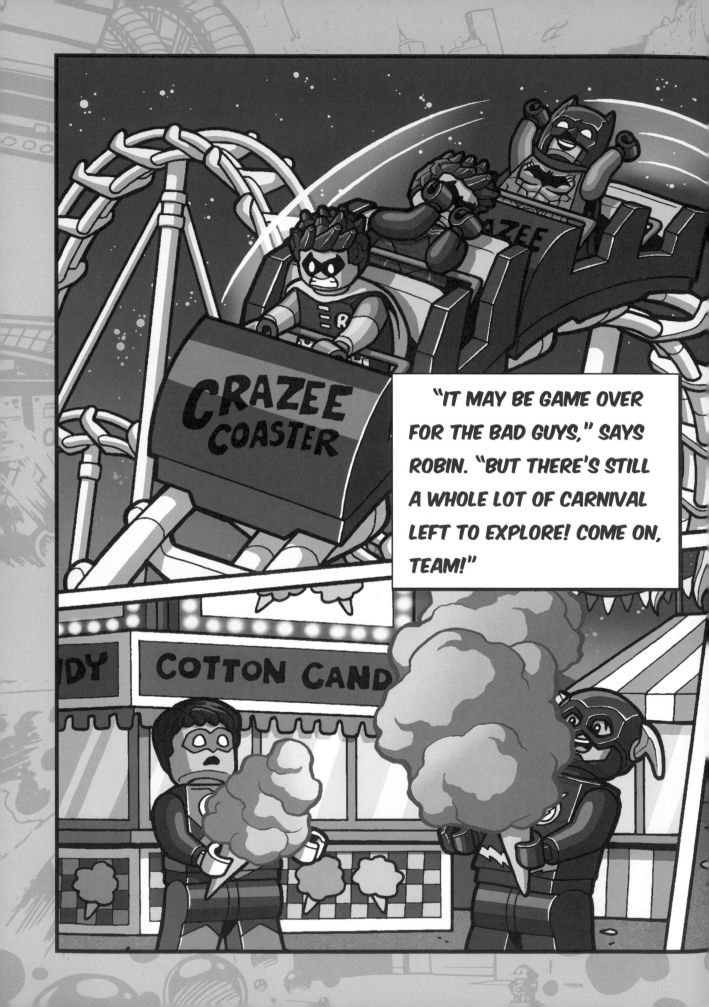

THE SUPER HEROES AGREE—THERE'S NO BETTER WAY TO CAP OFF A DAY OF CRIME FIGHTING THAN WITH SOME GOOD OLD-FASHIONED CARNIVAL FUN!

THE END.

FOLLOW THE CLUES

WHOOSH! WHAT'S THAT UP IN THE SKY?
IT'S BATMAN FLYING IN THE BATPLANE!

THE CAPED CRUSADER GOT A TIP FROM COMMISSIONER
GORDON THAT THE JOKER AND THE RIDDLER ARE
CAUSING MISCHIEF DOWNTOWN. WHAT COULD THOSE TWO
PRANKSTERS BE UP TO THIS TIME?

147

"THE PEOPLE OF GOTHAM CITY ARE ALL ASLEEP IN THEIR BEDS." THE JOKER LAUGHS AS HE FLIES HIS HELICOPTER.

"YOU CAN'T STOP WHAT YOU CAN'T CATCH!" CRIES THE JOKER. HE RELEASES AN EMERGENCY ROPE LADDER FROM HIS HELICOPTER AND STARTS TO ESCAPE!

BUT BATMAN THINKS FAST AND USES A MISSILE TO BREAK THE ROPE.

FWOOM! HE LANDS ON A COMFY MATTRESS THAT HE SET OUT EARLIER TO MAKE HIS ESCAPE ON!

"I'LL JUST CLEAR AWAY THIS SLEEP SMOKE WHILE YOU CATCH SOME ZS, JOKER," SAYS BATMAN.

"ZZZZZZZZ," SNORES THE JOKER.

"THAT'S ONE CROOK DOWN," SAYS BATMAN. "BUT COMMISSIONER GORDON SAID THE RIDDLER WAS UP TO HIS OLD TRICKS, TOO. WHERE COULD HE BE?"

SUDDENLY, BATMAN SPOTS A NOTE ON THE GROUND. IT'S FROM THE RIDDLER!

"I'VE GOT THE GUY IN BLUE," IT SAYS. "DO YOU WANT HIM BACK? YOU KNOW WHAT TO DO. LOOK FOR ME AND GET MY CLUES."

JUST THEN, ROBIN RUNS UP. "I CAME AS QUICK AS I
COULD. HAVE YOU FOUND THE RIDDLER?"

"NOT YET," SAYS BATMAN. "BUT HE LEFT A CLUE."

"YOU MEAN THIS ONE?" ROBIN CATCHES A PIECE OF PAPER FLOATING DOWN FROM ABOVE.

"NO, THAT'S A SECOND CLUE!" CRIES BATMAN. "WHAT DOES IT SAY?"

ROBIN READS THE NOTE. "BLUE BOY THINKS HE'S SUPER WHEN HE FLIES. BUT A BIT OF KRYPTONITE MAKES HIM DIVE."

"HE'S GOT SUPERMAN!" CRIES ROBIN. "BUT WHERE IS HE? AND WHAT'S HIS PLAN?"

LITTLE DO BATMAN AND ROBIN REALIZE, THE SNEAKY RIDDLER IS WATCHING THEM FROM ABOVE.

"HO, HO, HO!" THE RIDDLER LAUGHS. "THOSE DYNAMIC DO-GOODERS THINK THEY'RE SO CLEVER. WE'LL JUST SEE IF THEY'RE CLEVER ENOUGH TO REACH THEIR FRIEND IN TIME!"

THE RIDDLER DROPS DOWN SEVERAL MORE CLUE NOTES TO BATMAN AND ROBIN BEFORE SNEAKING BACK TO HIS HIDEOUT.

"STILL STUCK? SUPERMAN IS, TOO. AND IF YOU DON'T HURRY, HE'LL MEET HIS DOOM.

"FIND THE TIME, AND YOU'LL GET THE CLUE. TICKTOCK, TICKTOCK, TEN MINUTES 'TIL BOOM!"

"I GET THAT CLUE!" EXCLAIMS BATMAN. "SUPERMAN IS TRAPPED ON THE GOTHAM CITY CLOCK TOWER."

"AND WE ONLY HAVE TEN MINUTES," SAYS ROBIN. "LET'S GO!

BATMAN AND ROBIN FLY TO THE GOTHAM CITY CLOCK
TOWER.

"THANK GOODNESS YOU'RE HERE!" CRIES SUPERMAN.
"THE RIDDLER HAS ME TRAPPED IN THIS KRYPTONITE
GLUE!"

"NOTHING THE BATPLANE CLAW CAN'T HANDLE!" SAYS
BATMAN.

THEY FREE THEIR FRIEND AND SHUT OFF THE KRYPTONITE
BOMB JUST IN TIME!

"NOW TO CATCH THE RIDDLER," SAYS BATMAN. "AND I
HAVE JUST THE CLUE TO HELP US."

THE SUPER HEROES FOLLOW THE TRAIL OF PAPER CLUES LEFT ALL OVER GOTHAM CITY STRAIGHT TO THE RIDDLER'S HIDEOUT!

"CURSES!" CRIES THE RIDDLER. "HOW DID YOU FIND ME?"

"YOU TOLD US TO FOLLOW THE CLUES," SAYS BATMAN. "AND WE DID . . . STRAIGHT TO YOU!"

THE END.

SPACE JUSTICE

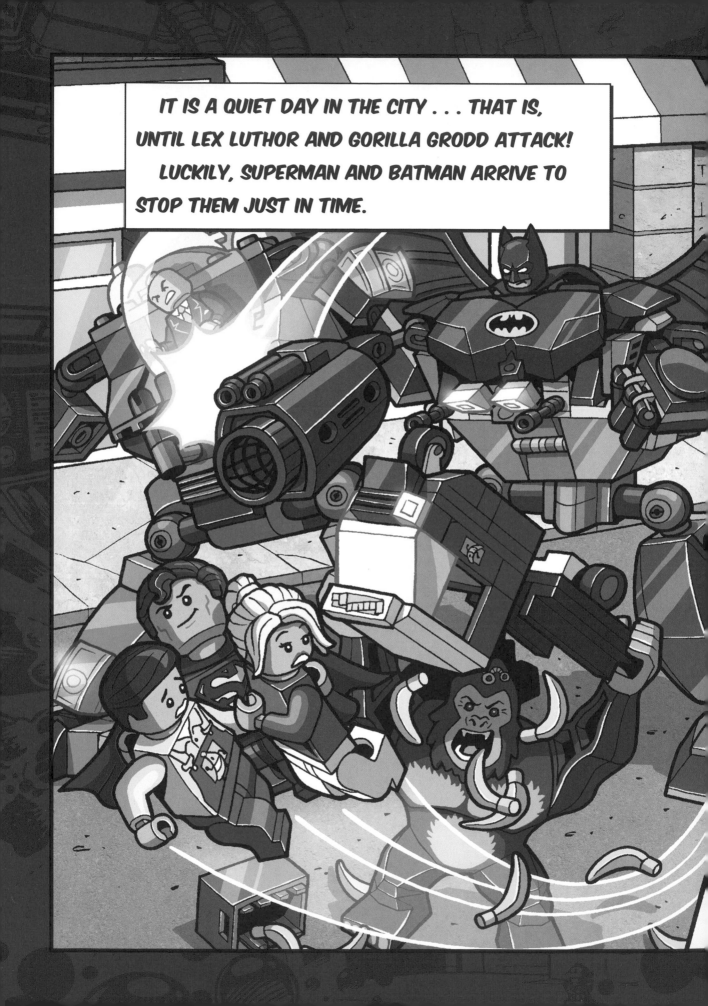

"YOU SHOULD HAVE MADE LIKE A BANANA AND SPLIT," SUPERMAN TEASES THE SUPER-VILLAINS.

"AND YOU SHOULD LEAVE THE BAD JOKES TO THE JOKER," SAYS BATMAN.

MEANWHILE, THE OTHER SUPER HEROES ARE BACK AT THEIR SECRET HEADQUARTERS. WHEN THEY AREN'T FIGHTING BAD GUYS, THEY LIKE TO HANG OUT AND WATCH MOVIES.

BUT SUPERMAN AND BATMAN DON'T WANT TO WATCH A MOVIE. THEY WANT A DAY OFF!

"WE'RE LEAVING YOU IN CHARGE," SUPERMAN TELLS THE REST OF THE TEAM. "IF THERE'S AN EMERGENCY, REMEMBER, ALWAYS HAVE A PLAN."

"HAS ANYONE SEEN MY BEACH UMBRELLA?" ASKS BATMAN.

BATMAN AND SUPERMAN HEAD TO THE BEACH. SUDDENLY, THE HEROES' MOVIE IS CUT OFF BY A MESSAGE FROM THREE SPACE VILLAINS: DARKSEID, SINESTRO, AND BRAINIAC!

"WE WILL ATTACK YOUR PLANET UNLESS EVERYONE ON EARTH SENDS US ALL THEIR TOYS!" THEY SAY.

"WE NEED TO BE SMART ABOUT THIS. LET'S COME UP WITH A PLAN," SAYS WONDER WOMAN.

BUT HAWKMAN, GREEN ARROW, AND MARTIAN MANHUNTER DECIDE THEY NEED TO TAKE ACTION RIGHT AWAY! THEY WANT TO ATTACK THE VILLAINS WITHOUT THINKING AHEAD.

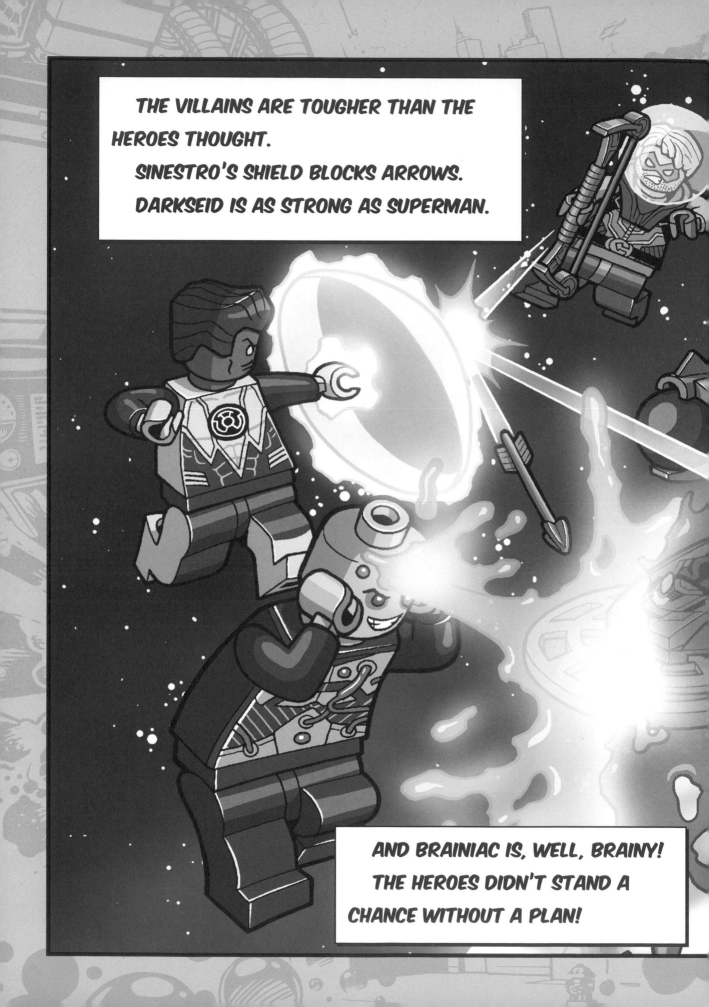

SUPERGIRL, WONDER WOMAN, AND BATGIRL WILL!
"IT LOOKS LIKE IT'S UP TO US," SAYS SUPERGIRL.

"BUT FIRST, WE NEED A PLAN," SAYS BATGIRL.

SUPERGIRL, WONDER WOMAN, AND BATGIRL COME UP WITH A *VERY* CLEVER PLAN.

"THEY'LL NEVER SEE US COMING!" SAYS BATGIRL.

BEFORE THEY LEAVE, WONDER WOMAN WRITES A NOTE ON THE FRIDGE. IT LETS THE OTHER HEROES KNOW WHERE THEY'VE GONE.

THEN THEY FLY OFF TO OUTER SPACE TO SAVE THEIR FRIENDS, THE WORLD, AND—OF COURSE—ALL THE TOYS!

FIRST, BATGIRL PUTS ON A DISGUISE. SHE DELIVERS A MYSTERIOUS BOX TO DARKSEID.

"SPECIAL DELIVERY," SHE SAYS IN A DEEP VOICE.

"FOR ME?" CRIES DARKSEID.

WHEN THE SPACE ALIEN OPENS THE BOX, HE GETS A
HERO-SIZED SURPRISE!

EVERYTHING IS GOING ACCORDING TO PLAN.

NEXT, SUPERGIRL PUTS A SHEET OVER HER HEAD AND SNEAKS UP ON SINESTRO.

"ACK!" CRIES SINESTRO. "A GHOST!"

WHEN SINESTRO GETS SCARED, HIS RING LOSES ITS POWER.

"SORRY, BUT YOU'RE TOO LATE," SAYS SUPERGIRL.
"THE VILLAINS HAVE ALREADY BEEN DEFEATED."
WAIT . . . WEREN'T THERE *THREE* SPACE VILLAINS?

BRAINIAC CRASHES INTO THE ROOM IN HIS SKULL SHIP!

"YOUR TIME IS UP," HE SHOUTS. "WE WILL ATTACK EARTH AND TAKE ALL THE TOYS!"

"NOT IF WE CAN HELP IT!" SAYS WONDER WOMAN.

WORKING TOGETHER, THE HEROES USE THEIR BRAINS AND MUSCLES TO DEFEAT BRAINIAC.

NOW ALL THE SPACE VILLAINS HAVE BEEN CAPTURED!

"ARE THERE TOYS IN SPACE JAIL?" DARKSEID ASKS.

"ONLY IF YOU BEHAVE," SAYS GREEN LANTERN.

WHEN THE HEROES GET HOME, THEY NEED A GOOD REST. HAVING A SPACE ADVENTURE AND SAVING THE WORLD IS HARD WORK!

LATER, SUPERMAN AND BATMAN RETURN FROM THEIR DAY AT THE BEACH. "EVERYONE'S ASLEEP," SAYS SUPERMAN. "I GUESS THERE WEREN'T ANY EMERGENCIES TODAY."

"I COULD USE SOME SLEEP MYSELF," SAYS BATMAN.
SUPERMAN AGREES. "NOW *THAT'S* A SMART PLAN."

THE END.